LET'S TRY
HORSEBACK RIDING

By Susa Hämmerle

Illustrated by Kyrima Trapp

Translated by Marisa Miller

NORTHSOUTH
BOOKS

New York / London

Rebecca was so excited. It was her birthday, and she couldn't wait to find out if she'd get the present she wanted most of all—riding lessons. And preferably on a big, black horse.

"Happy birthday to you, you live in a zoo . . ." roared her little brother, Jack. Her parents came in to wish her a happy birthday and Rebecca peeked eagerly at the presents. Could there be something horsey inside one of those packages?

Rebecca tore the wrapping paper off the presents. First, she got a book. Then she got a T-shirt. But so far, there were no horse presents. Rebecca was starting to get a lump in her throat, when she saw the carrots.

CARROTS?

What an odd present! She didn't even like carrots. Did they think she was a rabbit? Wait a minute—horses! Horses like to eat carrots!

Dad nodded. Mom smiled. And then Rebecca discovered a little card hidden in the bag of carrots. It was a gift certificate for ten riding lessons!

Yahoo!
Giddyap!
Yippee-ki-ay!

"Yahoo! Giddyap! Yippee-ki-ay!" Rebecca cried happily as she jumped for joy all around the room.

The stable was on a hill. Horses grazed in fenced meadows around the stable. A girl was taking a riding lesson in one of the rings. She trotted in circles on a pony, sitting as stiffly as if she'd swallowed a broomstick. Rebecca giggled. Soon she'd be trotting and galloping, too, but of course she'd be on a much bigger horse!

She still couldn't believe that she was actually going to be taking riding lessons. But it was no dream—here she was at the stables wearing riding breeches, boots, and a brand-new helmet, with her mom and Jack. The only thing that didn't belong in this picture was Jack. "Hey, stop swiping the carrots!" Rebecca hissed at him. "Those are for my horse!"

Just then, the riding instructor came over and introduced herself. Her name was Lucy, and she led them into the stable.

"*Mmmmmm*, the stable smells so good," said Rebecca. "Like hay and warmth and dust and—"

"Horse poop! *Ewwww!*" added Jack.

Rebecca ignored him. Her heart was pounding in excitement as she walked along the stalls.

"That's Nick," said Lucy. "And this is Orlando, a chestnut . . . are you all right, Rebecca?"

Rebecca didn't answer. She was staring at Nick's huge teeth, which he bared ferociously at her.

"Hey, let go! Give those back now!" Rebecca could hear Jack shouting at the other end of the stable. He was standing in front of the last stall playing tug-of-war with a pony over the bag of carrots.

"She may be greedy, but she's gentle as a lamb. Rebecca, you are going to learn to ride on Connie."

Pop! Rebecca's dream of riding on a big, black horse burst. She swallowed. Then she took another glance at Nick's teeth and walked over to Connie in relief.

Connie really was a sweet pony. For the first carrot, she let Rebecca pet her on the nose. For the second carrot, she let Rebecca stroke her mane. For the third carrot, she let Rebecca pat her on the neck. Rebecca stopped counting and followed Lucy into the stall.

Jack followed, too.

"Look at that funny, tangled tail," said Mom, taking two steps toward Connie's tail.

"Mom, everyone knows that you should never approach a horse from behind!" warned Rebecca sternly. "She could get frightened and kick you. Watch—this is how to do it!" Rebecca approached Connie slowly on her left side and spoke to her, "Hello, Connie. I'm Rebecca, and I'm going to ride you!"

"You know a lot already. Would you like to help me with saddling and bridling?" asked Lucy.

Rebecca didn't need to be asked twice. Eagerly, Rebecca fetched the saddle pad. Lucy laid it on Connie's back. On top of the pad went the saddle with its stirrups. Lucy tugged the girth snugly around Connie's belly.

"All right," she said, "now we need the bridle."

Oh boy! So much to do! Where was Jack? Rebecca looked around for him, hoping that he would help her.

There he was, trying to get on the saddle stand. First he tried to wiggle on from the front, then from the back, and then from the side until—thud—he landed on the ground.

Even Mom had to laugh as she helped him onto the wooden "horse."

"Yahoo! Giddyap!!!" cried Jack.

Rebecca thought this was very childish. She turned back to Connie. But what did she see? That greedy pony was gleefully chomping on carrot number who knows?

Lucy scolded Connie. Then she put the carrots in Jack's hand and the rope in Rebecca's hand. And presto! With an experienced grip, she slipped the bridle over Connie's head.

"Okay," said Lucy. "You're ready to lead Connie to the ring. Hold the rope loosely in your hand and walk right beside me. Make sure you keep a safe distance from her back hooves." It went very smoothly. Mom and Jack followed along after Connie.

When they reached the ring, Lucy made a stepladder with her hands to help Rebecca climb up. On the first try it didn't work. But once Lucy explained how to put one foot in the stirrup and then swing the other leg over the horse's back, Bingo! Rebecca was sitting in the saddle—just like a real horseback rider.

Jack was impressed. Rebecca gripped the front of the saddle tightly.

   Lucy unhooked the lead and fastened a long rope to the bridle. "This is the
lunge line," she explained. "I'll lead Connie around in circles. That way you
can get used to her movements."

   Clip, clop! Clip, clop! Rebecca felt as though she were on a swaying ship.
But before long, she felt quite steady.

Lucy even had her practice some tricks:

- First she had to hold on with only one hand.
- Then she had to hold on with her legs and no hands.
- Next she made a windmill with one arm.
- Finally, Lucy told her to reach for Connie's ears.

"Good job." Lucy praised Rebecca. "You'll make a good vaulter. Just watch Fiona."
Lucy pointed at the neighboring pen. There, a girl knelt on the back of a white horse,
holding her leg and her arm stretched out into the air.

"That exercise is called the flag," said Lucy. "And now Fiona's doing the mill." Rebecca was impressed. She kept looking over at Fiona, who was now standing on the horse's back!

Suddenly, Connie's head went down and she stopped with a lurch. Rebecca slid forward, grabbed Connie's mane, and wound up sitting on Connie's neck!

Mom was frightened and let out a cry. Lucy, however, remained calm. "Well, that's not exactly the best way to dismount," she said with a smile, and gently helped Rebecca down.

Rebecca's knees trembled.

Ah ha! It was a carrot, of course. Jack had tossed it right in front of Connie's hoof. And Connie had to stop to eat it, right away.

Lucy explained to Jack that you should never feed a horse during a lesson. It's best to save your treats for afterward, when the bridle is taken off, and the horse is being groomed and cleaned.

Grooming was what Rebecca had looked forward to most of all. Once they were back in the stable, Lucy went over all the cleaning tools. And then Rebecca was allowed to groom Connie, comb her mane, and scrape out her hooves. While she was being groomed, Connie happily munched the last of the carrots.

rubber currycomb

mud brush

mane and tail comb

dandy brush

hoof pick

sponge

"Well, you greedy girl," laughed Rebecca, "you ate the whole bag!" She patted the pony's neck. "But I'll be back next week. And then I'll bring you some apples."

Did Connie understand her? She snorted and grinned, showing off her long teeth as if she were already thinking about those apples . . .

There are many different kinds and colors of horses. Of course, you wouldn't find a horse as colorful as this one! But, you can use this horse to figure out the names of the different colors of horses by looking at their coats and their markings.

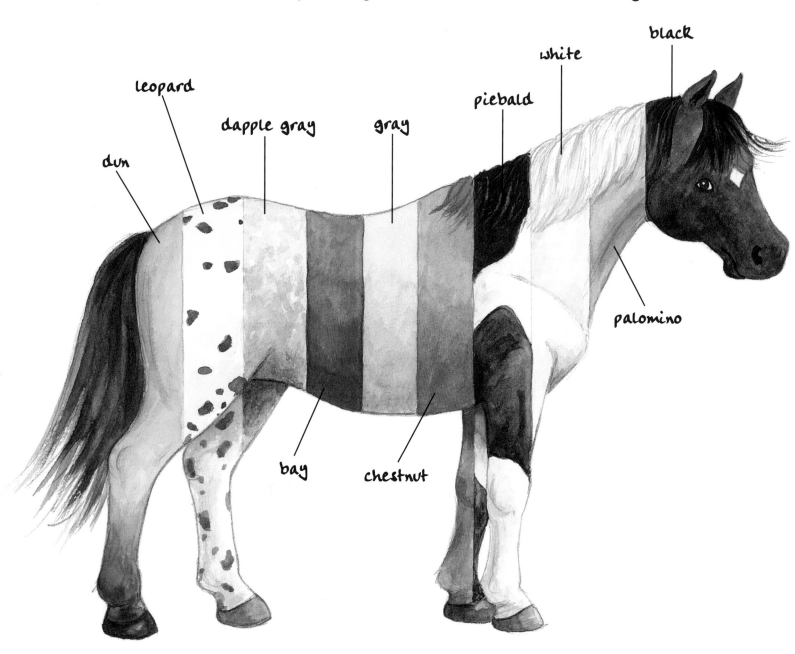

Horses don't just vary by color. They also come in different breeds. On the next page you can see a few of the most common ones.

Palomino

English Thoroughbred

Shetland
Pony

Andalusian

ipizzaner
(foals are born dark)

Friesian

Arabian

orwegian
rd Horse

Appaloosa

Barb

Pinto

Horses have always been considered noble animals. Their physiques are unique and well suited for running and jumping. Some of their body parts have funny names:

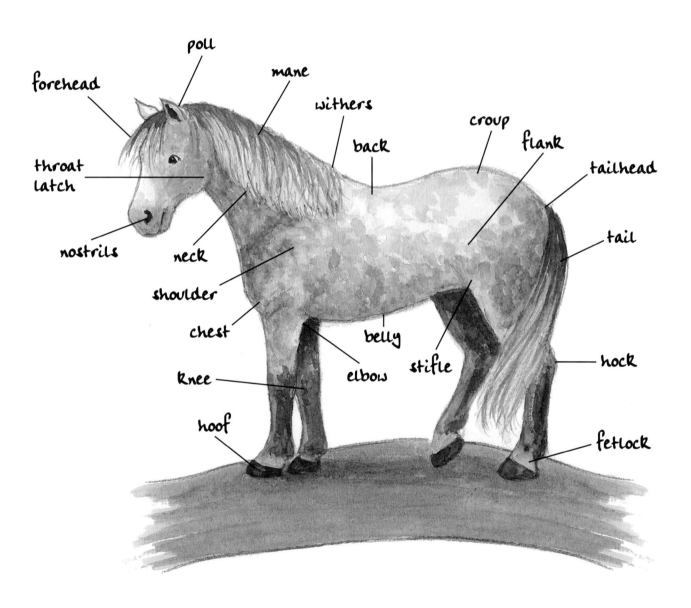

forehead
poll
mane
withers
back
croup
flank
tailhead
throat latch
nostrils
neck
shoulder
chest
belly
elbow
stifle
tail
knee
hoof
fetlock
hock

Horses wear special shoes called horseshoes. Some people believe that horseshoes bring good luck! There is a horseshoe hidden in this book. Can you find it?